FAVORITE MOTHER GOOSE RHYMES

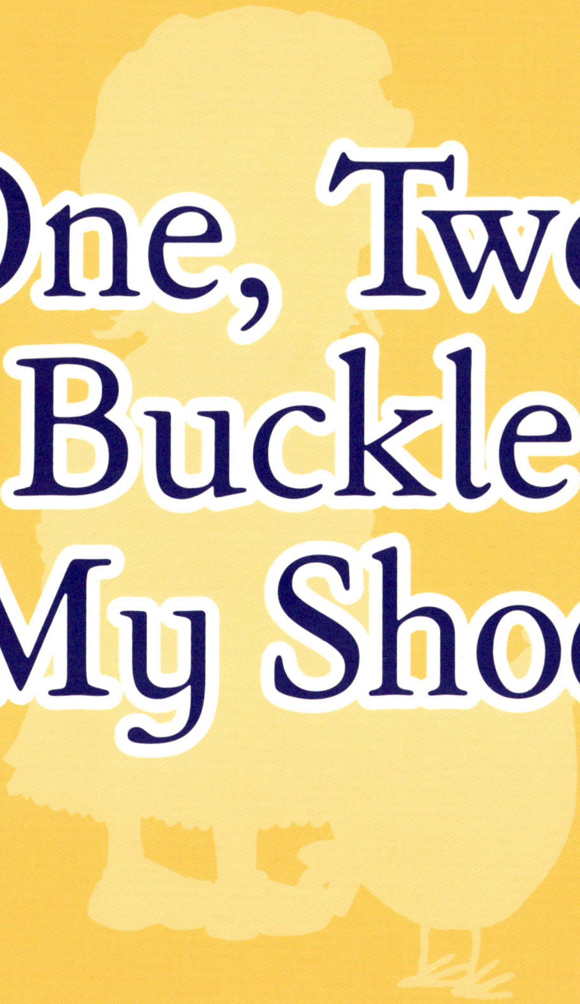

One, Two, Buckle My Shoe

The Child's World®

Published by The Child's World®
1980 Lookout Drive • Mankato, MN 56003-1705
800-599-READ • www.childsworld.com

Acknowledgments
The Child's World®: Mary Berendes, Publishing Director
Editorial Directions: E. Russell Primm, Editor; Lucia Raatma, Proofreader
The Design Lab: Kathleen Petelinsek, Art Direction and Design;
Anna Petelinsek and Victoria Stanley, Page Production

Library of Congress Cataloging-in-Publication Data
Billin-Frye, Paige.
One, two, buckle my shoe / illustrated by Paige Billin-Frye.
p. cm.— (Favorite Mother Goose rhymes)
Summary: An illustrated version of the traditional counting rhyme.
ISBN 978-1-60253-303-5 (library bound : alk. paper)
1. Nursery rhymes. 2. Children's poetry. [1. Nursery rhymes. 2. Counting.]
I. Mother Goose. II. Title. III. Series.
PZ8.3.B4945On 2009
398.8—dc22 2009001560

Printed in the United States of America
Mankato, Minnesota
May, 2010
PA02063

ILLUSTRATED BY PAIGE BILLIN-FRYE

One, two,
buckle my shoe.

Three, four,
shut the door.

Five, six,
pick up sticks.

Seven, eight,
lay them straight.

Nine, ten,
a good fat hen.

Eleven, twelve,
dig and delve.

Thirteen, fourteen,
maids a-courting.

Fifteen, sixteen,
maids in the kitchen.

Seventeen, eighteen,
maids a-waiting.

Nineteen, twenty,
my plate's empty.

ABOUT MOTHER GOOSE

We all remember the Mother Goose nursery rhymes we learned as children. But who was Mother Goose, anyway? Did she even exist? The answer is . . . we don't know! Many different tales surround this famous name.

Some people think she might be based on Goose-footed Bertha, a kindly old woman in French legend who told stories to children. The inspiration for this legend might have been Queen Bertha of France, who died in 783 and whose son Charlemagne ruled much of Europe. Queen Bertha was called Big-footed Bertha or Queen Goosefoot because one foot was larger than the other.

The name "Mother Goose" first appeared in Charles Perrault's *Les Contes de ma Mère l'Oye* ("Tales of My Mother Goose"), published in France in 1697. This was a collection of fairy tales including "Cinderella" and "Sleeping Beauty"—but these were stories, not poems. The first published Mother Goose nursery rhymes appeared in England in 1781, as *Mother Goose's Melody; or Sonnets for the Cradle*. But some of the verses themselves are hundreds of years old, passed along by word of mouth.

Although we don't really know the origins of Mother Goose or her nursery rhymes, we *do* know that these timeless verses are beloved by children everywhere!

ABOUT THE ILLUSTRATOR

Paige Billin-Frye studied illustration and design at Washington University in St. Louis, Missouri, and graduated in 1981. Before she began illustrating children's books, Paige illustrated posters and magazine covers, and painted illustrations for greeting cards. Today, she works in a studio in the Takoma neighborhood of Washington, D.C., a few blocks from her house. Paige has illustrated more than thirty-five books for children.